Mother Osprey

Nursery Rhymes for Buoys and Gulls

Written by Lucy Nolan

Illustrated by Connie McLennan

To Angelina, who fell in love with the beach on her very first visit — LN

Thanks to Adm. Wright and the Texas Navy Association for the artwork reference for *Two Skippers from Texas* — CM

Publisher's Cataloging-In-Publication Data

Nolan, Lucy A.
Mother Osprey : nursery rhymes for buoys and gulls / written by Lucy Nolan ;
illustrated by Connie McLennan.
p. : col. ill. ; cm.

Summary: What if Jack and Jill had been playing on a nice soft sand dune instead of that treacherous hill? And suppose Mary's pet wasn't really a lamb? What if Mary had a little clam? This collection retells Mother Goose rhymes and celebrates America's coastlines and waterways from sea to shining sea. Includes "For Creative Minds" section.

Interest age level: 003-007.
Interest grade level: P-2.
Lexile Code: NP
ISBN: 978-1-934359-96-9 (hardcover)
ISBN: 978-1-607180-41-8 (pbk.)
ISBN: 978-1-607180-61-6 (English eBook)
ISBN: 978-1-607180-51-7 (Spanish eBook)

1. Ocean--Juvenile poetry. 2. Marine animals--Juvenile poetry. 3. Coasts--Juvenile poetry.
4. Mother Goose--Adaptations. 5. Nursery rhymes, American. 6. Ocean--Poetry. 7.
Marine animals--Poetry. 8. Coasts--Poetry. 9. Nursery rhymes. 10. American poetry. I.
McLennan, Connie. II. Title. III. Title: Mother Goose. Selections.
PZ8.3.N65 Mo 2009
398.8   2009922606

Printed in China

Sylvan Dell Publishing
976 Houston Northcutt Blvd., Suite 3
Mt. Pleasant, SC 29464

Mary Had a Little Clam

Mary had a little clam—
   its shell was white as snow.
And everywhere that Mary went,
   the clam was sure to go.

He followed her to school one day.
   He set out in September
but reached the school in mid July—
   clams cannot rush, remember?

Where were all the boys and girls
   to play with as he'd dreamed?
School was out for summer break—
   boy, was that clam steamed!

Jack & June

Jack and June went up a dune
 to see the big wide water;
Jack fell down and rolled around,
 and June came tumbling after.

Jack and June all afternoon
 did stay in constant motion;
used their pail to bail and bail,
 but couldn't drain the ocean.

Buoys & Gulls

What are little buoys made of, made of?
What are little buoys made of?
"A bell and a light that flashes at night,
that's what little buoys are made of."

What are little gulls made of, made of?
What are little gulls made of?
"Mischief and daring and one pickled herring,
that's what little gulls are made of."

Sing a Song of Sixpence

Sing a song of sixpence,
 a pocket full of hay;
four and twenty pelicans
 fixed a luncheon tray.

When the tray was finished,
 the birds knew what to do;
they set this very dainty dish
 before the trawler crew.

The first mate ate his sandwich
 while hauling in the catch;
the captain ate more slowly
 while sitting on the hatch.

The deckhand asked for seconds;
 it was his favorite dish:
a little peanut butter—
 and lots of jellyfish!

Row, Row, Row Your Boat

Row, row, row your boat.
Start in Biscayne Bay.
If you come upon a shark,
row the other way!

Row, row, row your boat.
Now the 'Glades begin.
Never touch a floating log
with a toothy grin!

Row, row, row your boat,
through the Florida Keys.
If a pirate asks to ride,
make sure that he says, "Please!"

Row, row, row your boat,
'round and 'round Key West.
Now your arms are surely tired;
stop and take a rest!

One Flamingo

One flamingo, two flamingo, three flamingo, four.
A flamboyance of flamingoes is a group of three or more.

First a goose, and then some geese—a gaggle in the lane.
But if the geese are flying, then the gaggle is a skein.

A band of roving jellyfish is called a smack—how odd!
And whales that swim together form a group that's called a pod.

Seagulls form a colony, and curlews form a herd.
But cormorants are called a gulp—they're such a silly bird.

A school of fish, a shoal of bass, a wriggly swarm of eels.
Call them anything you want—to me they sound like meals.

When puffins float together, then their group is called a raft.
And herrings make an army—have you heard a thing so daft?

Sardines form a tight-knit group—like Mom and Dad and me.
Perhaps that's why a sardine clan is called a family.

Hatteras Light Is Falling Down

Hatteras Light is falling down,
     falling down,
     falling down.
They tell me that she's losing ground,
my fair lady.

Build her up with wood and clay,
     wood and clay,
     wood and clay.
But wood and clay will wash away,
my fair lady.

Shore her up with mortar and bricks,
     mortar and bricks,
     mortar and bricks.
Mortar and bricks won't do the trick,
my fair lady.

Let's move her from the ocean's reach,
　　ocean's reach,
　　ocean's reach.
Half a mile beyond the beach,
my fair lady.

Everybody clear the way,
　　clear the way,
　　clear the way.
They tell me that it's moving day,
my fair lady.

Isn't that the strangest sight,
　　strangest sight,
　　strangest sight?
Down the road comes Hatteras Light
my fair lady.

Let the ocean crash and pound,
　　crash and pound,
　　crash and pound.
Hatteras Light is safe and sound,
my fair lady.

Ride a Wild Mare

Ride a wild mare
down the beach, if you dare,
to join the fat ponies gathered there.
I've heard they're the children of mares and stallions
who swam ashore from shipwrecked galleons.

An Old Woman who Lived in a Shell

There was an old woman who lived in a shell;
    she had too many children to fit very well.
So she added an attic and three or four sheds,
    to make room for all of the oyster beds.

Lobster Pies

Old Mrs. Wise
made lobster pies,
all on a winter's day;
her greedy son
grabbed every one
and took them clean away.

What a surprise
for Junior Wise
lay inside that croaker sack.
When he sat on a bench
to eat a pinch,
the lobster pies pinched back!

Lydia Gail

Lydia Gail has lost her whale.
He's somewhere around Nantucket.
Leave him alone, and he'll make himself known.
(He's hiding in her bucket.)

The Witch of November, 1913

Do you remember
    the storm of November?
Howling wind, high seas, and snow.
    A change in the air
    caught the ships unaware
    and roused the witch below.
The season's last load
    of cargo was stowed.
Howling wind, high seas and snow.
    But the grain and the ore
    would never see shore.
    How could the crewmen know?
No warnings were heard
    as the cauldron was stirred.
Howling wind, high seas and snow.
    Eight freighters were gone
    from Lake Huron alone
    as the witch let her fury go.

The overturned Price
      was shrouded with ice.
Howling wind, high seas and snow.
      The Argus, it's told,
      cracked apart from the cold
      in a sad and eerie show.
The lakes heaved and tossed—
      so many lives lost.
Howling wind, high seas and snow.
      More than two hundred souls
      filled those sorrowful rolls—
      the crewmen of long ago.
When the lakes are like glass,
      the memories pass.
Howling wind, high seas and snow.
      But always remember
      the Witch of November
      when autumn winds start to blow.

Sleep Baby Sleep

Sleep, baby sleep,
upon the river deep.
The Mississippi rolls along;
it hums a peaceful nighttime song.
Sleep, baby sleep.

Sleep, baby sleep,
the moonbeams dance and leap;
the paddle wheel sings and sighs,
it spins out gentle lullabies.
Sleep, baby sleep.

Sleep, baby sleep,
upon the river deep.
When morning comes, you'll be with me,
your cares will drift on out to sea.
Sleep, baby sleep.

Two Skippers from Texas

There once were two skippers from Texas,
who were both standing watch on their deckses.
When the two ships drew near,
neither skipper would veer.
So, except for a wheel,
and the bit of one keel,
the two ships are now just wreckses.

I Saw A Ship A-Sailing

I saw a ship a-sailing.
A-sailing on the sea,
a-sailing on a sea of grass
to where the land was free.

A family walked beside her,
just like sailors at the rail—
the gallant Prairie Schooner
drifting down the Oregon Trail.

There was salt pork in the barrels,
and apples in the hold.
The canvas bonnet crackled,
as the wheels creaked and rolled.

The schooner trundled onward,
through the wind and sun and rain.
Watch close! The Prairie Schooners
will not pass this way again.

Tweedle-Dum & Tweedle-Dee

Tweedle-dum and Tweedle-dee
one day went for a paddle.
They planned to see the okra pods
that swim just off Seattle.

They'd eaten okra many times;
they liked it in their gumbo.
They hoped to see a monstrous pod—
they hoped it would be jumbo.

But fourteen hours later,
killer whales were all they'd found.
Where were the pods of okra
that live in Puget Sound?

If Tweedle-dum and Tweedle-dee
could spell they'd know the score . . .
orcas frolic in the waves;
okra stays on shore.

Hark, Hark!

Hark, hark! The sea lions bark!
Who's that swimming by?
    There's a stranger about
    with a whiskery snout
    and a twinkle in his eye.

Who's there? The sea lions stare.
Who's that heading their way?
    Who misbehaves
    while making waves
    at Sea Lion Rocks today?

Oh, ho! I think I know
who's playing in the water.
    A mischievous clown
    splashing up and down
    just doing what he otter!

For Creative Minds

Mary Had a Little Clam

The muscular "foot" of a clam is used mainly for digging, but can sometimes be used for "creeping" or even "leaping" away from predators. Clams are bivalves; they have two shells attached by a hinge. Their shells grow with them as they grow— just as our bones grow as we do! Many people enjoy eating steamed clams—do you?

Jack & June

Some sand dunes just don't want to stay put! Jockey's Ridge, the largest sand dune on the East Coast, moves three to six feet a year, covering up everything that stands in its way. Sand dunes can be next to the ocean, lakes, in the desert, or even in the mountains!

Buoys & Gulls

Buoys mark deep water channels for boaters or mark fishing or lobster traps. Buoys can also be used to measure weather information.

As a black-headed laughing gull wheels through the air with a loud "ha-ha-ha," it sounds as if he's up to mischief. Perhaps he's delighted by his tasty diet of fish, garbage, sewage, and scraps from fishing boats!

Sing a Song of Sixpence

Don't ever let a brown pelican ask you to dinner. He might expect you to dive headfirst into the ocean, scoop up fish with your mouth, and then swallow them whole! Peanut butter is made from peanuts but jelly isn't made from jellyfish—it's made from fruit like grapes or strawberries.

Row, Row, Row Your Boat

While boating in the Everglades, you might bump into an alligator—or even an American crocodile! Alligators live in fresh water and have wide, U-shaped, rounded snouts. Crocodiles live in salt or brackish water and have longer, more pointed, V-shaped snouts.

One Flamingo

Animals groups have many different names: families, pods, skeins, herds, dens, flocks, and hordes are just a few.

Hatteras Light Is Falling Down

In 1999, the Cape Hatteras Lighthouse, the tallest lighthouse in the United States, was moved over half a mile inland to keep it from falling into the sea due to beach erosion. The move took 23 days.

An Old Woman who Lived in a Shell

Would you believe that oysters start off their lives footloose and fancy-free? Young oysters float around until they begin to grow a shell, then they drop to the bottom and form a reef with other oysters. It seems that when oysters meet, they grow quite attached to each other! An oyster "group" is called a "bed."

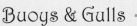

Lobster Pies

To avoid being eaten, a lobster should stay out of the kitchen—and the parlor. Lobstermen call the front of the lobster trap the kitchen, and the back is called the parlor! Lobsters found in New England have front claws with pinchers, unlike the Spanish lobsters found in southern waters.

Ride a Wild Mare

What do "saltwater cowboys" do each July? They round up ponies on Virginia's Assateague Island and herd them across the channel to Chincoteague for the volunteer fire department's pony auction. The ponies that aren't sold swim back home. Wild horses also live on North Carolina's Outer Banks and Georgia's Cumberland Island and are believed to be descendants of horses that survived shipwrecks by swimming ashore.

Lydia Gail

Legend says the Indian giant Maushop dumped the sand out of his moccasin to form Nantucket Island. What happened to the sand from his other moccasin? That became Martha's Vineyard. Both islands are part of Cape Cod.

The Witch of November, 1913

Violent autumn storms that batter the Great Lakes are called "November Witches" or "White Hurricanes." The Great Storm of 1913 killed over 270 people and sank 12 ships, only seven of which have been found. Another November Witch sank the Edmund Fitzgerald in 1975.

Sleep Baby Sleep

Just how fast does the Mississippi flow? A raindrop falling on the headwaters in Lake Itasca, Minnesota, would take about 90 days or three months to travel the 2,350 miles (3,781 km) to the Gulf of Mexico. The invention of the steamboat changed transportation of people and products! Now ships could go upriver as easily as they could go downriver.

Two Skippers from Texas

Did you know Texas once had its own Navy? Of the four original ships, one was wrecked in a storm, one was wrecked in battle, one was captured by Mexico, and one was sold because the Republic of Texas couldn't pay for repairs!

I Saw A Ship A-Sailing

Covered wagons were sometimes called prairie schooners, and a schooner is a type of sailboat. Pioneers often chose to walk beside their wagons—and it's no wonder; it is said that the ride was so bumpy, a bucket of milk could churn itself into butter before the day was done.

Tweedle-Dum & Tweedle-Dee

Despite its massive size, an orca killer whale is quite agile and can reach speeds of 30 miles per hour. The vegetable, okra, on the other hand, grows in gardens!

Hark, Hark!

Even the most rambunctious sea otter has to sleep sometime. So how does he keep from drifting away from his family? He wraps himself in the long strands of kelp that are anchored to the sea floor. Sea otters can be found in the Pacific Ocean but not the Atlantic Ocean.

Twinkle, Twinkle

Most people think of asteroids circling the sun. But did you know that "asteroid" is also the scientific name for most common sea stars?

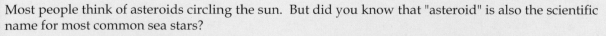

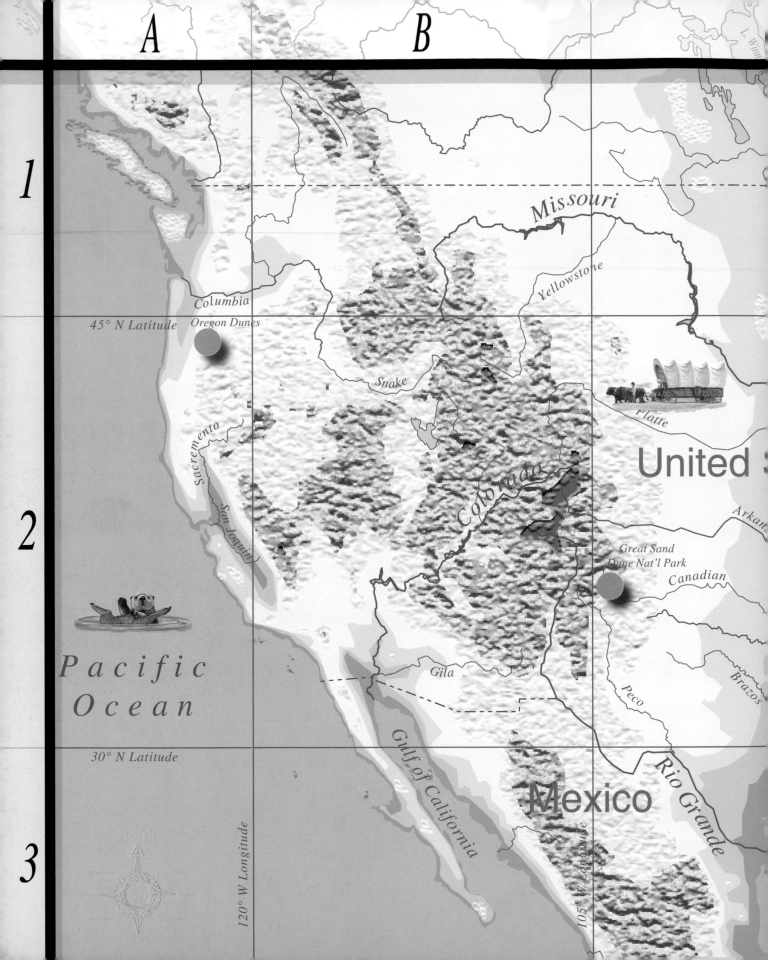

A

B

1

2

3

Missouri

Yellowstone

Columbia

45° N Latitude
Oregon Dunes

Snake

Sacramento

San Joaquin

Platte

Colorado

United S

Arkan

Great Sand
Dune Nat'l Park

Canadian

Pacific
Ocean

Gila

Peco

Brazos

30° N Latitude

Gulf of California

Rio Grande

Mexico

North

120° W Longitude

105° W Longitude

L. Winn

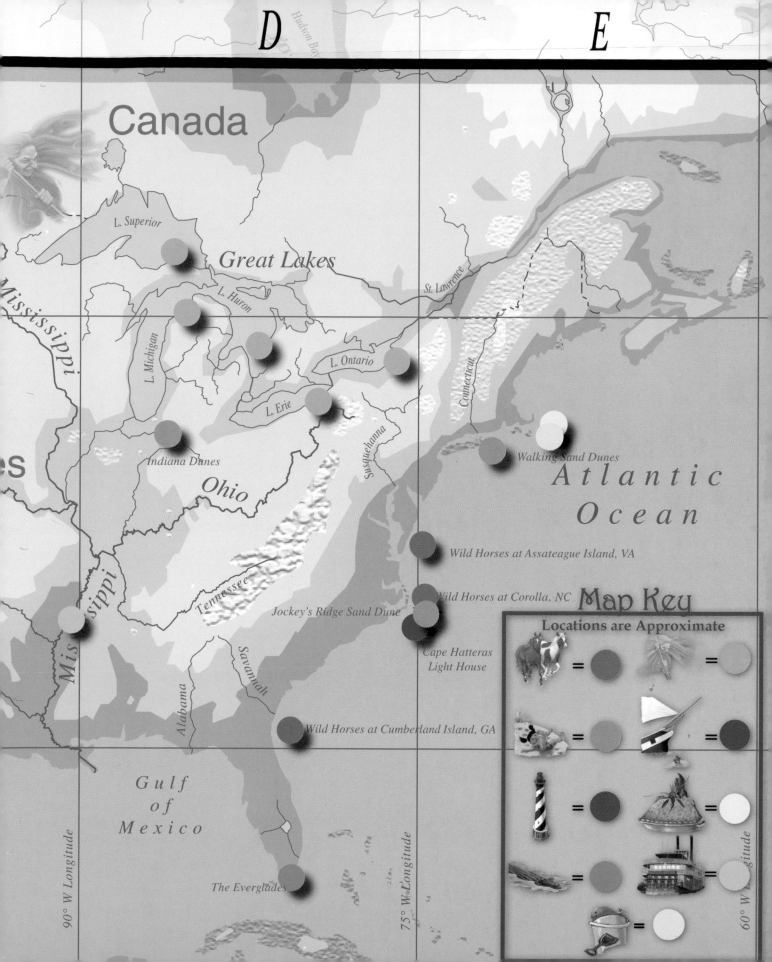

Canada

L. Superior

Great Lakes

L. Huron

St. Lawrence

Mississippi

L. Michigan

L. Ontario

L. Erie

Connecticut

Indiana Dunes

Ohio

Susquehanna

Atlantic
Ocean

Walking Sand Dunes

Tennessee

Wild Horses at Assateague Island, VA

Mississippi

Wild Horses at Corolla, NC

Map Key

Jockey's Ridge Sand Dune

Alabama

Savannah

Cape Hatteras
Light House

Wild Horses at Cumberland Island, GA

Gulf
of
Mexico

The Everglades

90° W Longitude

75° W Longitude

60° W Longitude

Locations are Approximate

Map Activity Questions

Use the map and compass rose to answer the following questions. Answers are upside down on the bottom of the page.

1. What is the name of the country north of the United States?

2. What is the name of the country south of the United States?

3. Are the Great Lakes north or south of the Gulf of Mexico?

4. Is Nantucket (represented by Lydia Gail's bucket) on the East or West Coast of the United States?

5. Find the covered wagon on the map. What are the grid coordinates?

6. Find the Everglades (represented by the crocodile) on the map. What are the grid coordinates?

7. Find the Cape Hatteras Lighthouse on the map. What are the grid coordinates?

8. In which direction would you have to go to travel from the Florida Everglades to see the Cape Hatteras lighthouse?

9. Is the sea otter in the Atlantic or Pacific Ocean?

10. Into what body of water does the Mississippi River flow?

11. How many sand dunes are marked on the map? Are they all by the ocean?

12. How many Great Lakes are there, and what are their names?

Poem-Related Questions

1. How long did it take Mary's clam to get to school (September to July)? Why do you think it took so long?

2. Why do you think the Hatteras Lighthouse started falling down? Do you think it was easy to move it? Why or why not?

3. Would an old lady living in a shell use oyster beds? What are oyster beds? Would you like to sleep on one?

4. What do you think the "Witch of November, 1913" was?

5. What type of "ship" sailed across the prairies?

Food for Thought

The poems relate in some way to water: oceans, bays, lakes, or rivers. Why do you think water is so important to us?

How did people in history (natives and early settlers) use water?

Do we use it in the same way today?

Poem-Related Answers: 1: nine months, clams don't move very quickly; 2: beach erosion; 3: the place where oysters grow; 4: a violent storm that can be near hurricane force; 5: covered wagons.

Map Activity Answers: 1: Canada; 2: Mexico; 3: north; 4: east; 5: 2C; 6: 3D; 7: 2D; 8: northeast; 9: Pacific Ocean; 10: Gulf of Mexico; 11: 5 - no; 12: 5 - Lakes Superior, Huron, Michigan, Erie, & Ontario